WANDA'S ROSES

B Y P A T B R I S S O N

I L L U S T R A T E D B Y M A R Y A N N C O C C A - L E F F L E R

BOYDS MILLS PRESS

HONESDALE, PENNSYLVANIA

Boyds Mills Press, Inc.
815 Church Street
Honesdale, Pennsylvania 18431
Printed in the United States of America

Publisher Cataloging-in-Publication Data
Brisson, Pat.
Wanda's roses / by Pat Brisson ; illustrated by Maryann Cocca-Leffler.
—1st ed.
[32]p. : col. ill. ; cm.
Summary: Wanda mistakes a thornbush for a rosebush in the empty lot. She clears away the trash
around it and cares for it every day, even though no roses bloom.
ISBN: 978-1-56397-136-5 (hc) • ISBN: 978-1-56397-925-5 (pb)

1. Inner cities—Fiction—Juvenile literature. 2. Neighborhood—Fiction—
Juvenile literature. [1. Inner cities—Fiction. 2. Neighborhood—Fiction.]
I. Cocca-Leffler, Maryann, ill. II. Title.
[E]   1994   CIP
Library of Congress Catalog Card Number 93-72916

First edition
First Boyds Mills Press paperback edition, 2000
Book designed by Maryann Cocca-Leffler
A special thanks to Matt Ralph
The text of this book is set in Stone Serif.
The illustrations are done in gouache and colored pencil.

20 19 18 17 16

For Elvira
who loves roses,
and for everyone
who believes in a
dream
        —PB

To my mother,
Rose
      Love,
      Maryann

One morning in May on the way to school, Wanda noticed a bush growing in the empty corner lot at Fillmore and Hudson streets. It must have been growing for a while because it was about two feet tall, and Wanda was surprised she hadn't noticed it before. But there it was—bare and thorny—and Wanda, who loved beautiful things, felt her heart beat faster.

"A rosebush!" she said to herself. *"My very own rosebush!"*

Now, the rosebush didn't really belong to Wanda, but since nobody seemed to own the lot or the heaps of junk that were piled there, she decided she would care for this bush and make it her own.

All during school she thought about her rosebush. During Art she drew pictures of what it would look like in bloom.

During Library she borrowed books on arranging flowers.

During Science she asked so many questions about how to take care of it that finally her teacher said she really must stop asking questions about roses and start thinking about electricity, which was what the lesson was about.

After school she rushed to the rosebush. It was still bare and thorny.

Maybe it needs some more sun, thought Wanda. So she put down her schoolbag and began dragging some of the nearby trash out to the curb. Mrs. Turner, who was on her way to the store, stopped to help her with a broken chair.

"Cleaning up the neighborhood, Wanda?" Mrs. Turner asked. "That's a nice project for you."

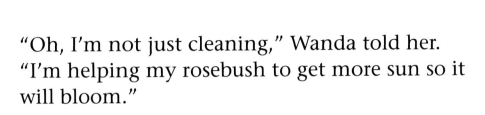

"Oh, I'm not just cleaning," Wanda told her. "I'm helping my rosebush to get more sun so it will bloom."

"Your rosebush?" Mrs. Turner asked. "Where is your rosebush?"

"Over there," Wanda said, pointing proudly to the bare, thorny bush.

"Oh, Wanda, I'm not so sure that's a rosebush," Mrs. Turner said gently.

"Sure it is," said Wanda. "I've seen rosebushes in books, and this is what they look like before they bloom. You just wait . . . in a few weeks this lot will be full of roses."

"Well," said Mrs. Turner, shaking her head, "good luck with it, Wanda."

And as she walked away, Mrs. Turner thought to herself, If that's a rosebush, then I'm the queen of England.

The next day after school Wanda hurried to her rosebush.
It was still bare and thorny.

Maybe it needs more air, thought Wanda. So she put down
her schoolbag and began taking more of the trash out to
the curb.

Once I get all this trash out of here, nothing will block the
air from getting to my rosebush, Wanda thought.

Mr. Claudel was on his way home from work, saw Wanda trying to drag an old door, and stopped to help.

"Cleaning up the neighborhood, are you, Wanda?" he asked.

"Not just cleaning, Mr. Claudel," Wanda told him. "I'm getting rid of this trash so my rosebush will get more air."

"A rosebush? Here?" Mr. Claudel asked.

And so Wanda showed him the rosebush.

"I don't know much about gardening, Wanda,"
Mr. Claudel said, frowning, "but I don't think that's
a rosebush."

"Sure it is," said Wanda, "and in a few weeks this lot will
be filled with the sweetest-smelling roses you ever saw."

She thanked Mr. Claudel for his help and went off to drag
away some more trash.

Mr. Claudel shook his head. "If that's a rosebush," he said
to himself, "then I'm the king of France."

Every day after school that week and the next,
Wanda worked in the empty lot. Mrs. Giamoni, who
lived in an apartment next door, gave Wanda trash bags
for the old shoes, beer bottles, broken toys, and bits of glass
that she was picking up.

"You've done a great job cleaning up this lot, Wanda," Mrs. Giamoni told her.

"Oh, I'm not just cleaning," Wanda said. "I have to get rid of all this trash so my rosebush will get enough sun and fresh air to bloom."

"But where is your rosebush?" Mrs. Giamoni asked.

So Wanda showed her.

Mrs. Giamoni put her hand on Wanda's shoulder
and spoke softly to her. "Wanda," she said,
"this is not a rosebush."

"Oh, but it is," said Wanda. "And in a few weeks this lot
will be filled with the most beautiful roses you ever saw."

"That would be nice," said Mrs. Giamoni. "But I don't
want you to be disappointed if this bush doesn't bloom."

"Don't worry, Mrs. Giamoni," Wanda answered.
"I won't be disappointed."

Mrs. Giamoni sighed. That is not a rosebush
and will never be one,
she thought to
herself.

The next week, when the rosebush still wasn't blooming, Wanda talked to her school librarian. "I need some books about getting roses to bloom," she told Ms. Jones.

"Oh, do you have a rosebush, Wanda?" Ms. Jones asked.

"Yes, but it doesn't have flowers yet, and I know it has enough sun and fresh air."

"Does it have enough water?" Ms. Jones asked.

"Water!" Wanda said. "Of course! That will make it bloom."

That afternoon she hurried to the rosebush.
It was still bare and thorny. She looked
at the dry ground and smiled.

"Don't worry, little bush," she said
out loud. "I'll get you some
water, and then you'll be
able to grow flowers."

Wanda went to the butcher
shop across the street.

"Mr. Sanchez,
would you please
give me some water
for my rosebush?"

"Rosebush? Is that what I see you
taking care of and talking to every day
over there? Are you sure that's a rosebush,
Wanda?" Mr. Sanchez asked.

"Oh, yes, I'm sure," Wanda said. "But it can't bloom
because it needs water."

Mr. Sanchez gave her water in a plastic bucket.

"I hope that really is a rosebush, Wanda," he said, looking
at her doubtfully.

"You'll see," Wanda told him. "In a few weeks that
whole lot will be full of roses."

As Wanda carried the water to her rosebush
Mr. Sanchez muttered, "In a few weeks
that thornbush will still be a thornbush."

Every day Wanda ran to her rosebush after school, but every day it was still bare and thorny. She watered it and sang to it and checked its bare branches for roses.

Mr. Claudel, on his way home from work, stopped to see if there were any roses yet.

Mrs. Turner, on her way to the butcher shop, stopped to see if there were any roses yet.

Mrs. Giamoni, seeing Wanda in the lot, called down from her apartment to ask if there were any roses yet.

When Wanda went to the library at school, Ms. Jones asked if there were any roses yet.

And every day, when Wanda went to the butcher shop for water, Mr. Sanchez asked if there were any roses yet.

To each person Wanda would answer the same thing. "Just you wait . . . pretty soon this whole lot will be filled with roses."

And then one day in June, Wanda had an idea. Looking at the bare, thorny bush, she said, "If my rosebush won't give roses to me, I'll just have to give roses to my rosebush." And when she saw Mrs. Turner, Mr. Claudel, Mrs. Giamoni, Ms. Jones, and Mr. Sanchez, she gave each of them an invitation that said:

Please come
For Tea and
Muffins
In Wanda's
Rose Garden
Saturday
Morning
at 9

"Oh, dear," said Mrs. Turner. "Is she still expecting to get roses from that bush?"

"Oh, no," said Mr. Claudel. "And she's worked so hard, too. . . ."

"Oh, my," said Mrs. Giamoni. "She'll be so disappointed. . . ."

"Oh, darn," said Mr. Sanchez. "There must be something I can do. . . ."

"Oh, good," said Ms. Jones, who had only heard about the bush from Wanda and hadn't seen it for herself. "And I'll bring the muffins."

The night before the tea party everyone was very busy.
And the next morning at nine, everyone was surprised
to see Wanda's rosebush covered with roses—paper
roses that Wanda had made herself and carefully
tied to each bare, thorny branch.

But more surprising yet,

everyone who came to the party had brought along a rosebush to plant near

Wanda's (except Ms. Jones, who had brought delicious blueberry muffins).

After they had eaten their muffins and drunk their tea, they all got busy planting rosebushes. Mr. Claudel and Mrs. Turner dug the holes, Mrs. Giamoni held the bushes in place while Wanda and Ms. Jones filled in around the roots with soil, and Mr. Sanchez brought water from his shop and watered them all thoroughly.

When the work was finished, Mr. Claudel said, "Wanda, this is going to be a rose garden fit for a king!"

"Or a queen!" said Mrs. Turner.

Wanda and the others smiled.

And later that summer the whole lot was filled with the biggest, most beautiful, sweetest-smelling roses that anyone had ever seen—just as Wanda had always said it would be.